WALDEN
LANE

Ashley's Test

The Bet

Bigmouth

Halloween

Hike

Missing Money

The New Kid

Outdoor Ed Invasion

Shady Neighbors

Vandalism

SADDLEBACK
EDUCATIONAL PUBLISHING
www.sdlback.com

ISBN-13: 978-1-68021-368-3
ISBN-10: 1-68021-368-7
eBook: 978-1-63078-583-3

Printed in Malaysia

21 20 19 18 17   1 2 3 4 5

Missing Money

EVAN JACOBS

Cell Phone Zone

Steve loves zombie photo filters. Sick!

Thuy—killer of all things fun—loves to photobomb strangers.

Tyler follows Grumpy Cat's Twitter feed.

Principal Williams still uses a flip phone.

Chapter 1
Big Trip

Dude, the Viper looks sick!" Marlon Moore told Steve McCain. Marlon was excited.

The boys had their phones. They were video chatting.

Steve brushed his teeth.

Marlon was already in bed. He had his blanket. It was pulled up to his chest. His room was a mess. It was a mix of video games, clothes, and books. The lights were off.

Sunday nights were always a letdown. Five days of school were ahead.

"X2 looks way more gnarly," Steve said. Toothpaste foamed in his mouth.

They were talking about the eighth-grade trip. It happened every year. Eighth graders got to go to Magic Mountain. It was an amusement park.

Marlon and Steve were eighth graders. They went to Walden Lane Middle School. Walden Lane was a small city. It was surrounded by nature. There were hills and trails.

The city was like most others. There were beautiful homes in the wealthy parts. People rented when they couldn't afford to own. Some areas were nicer than others.

"Just think," Marlon said. "Three more weeks! Then we'll be there."

"I'm riding Colossus three times," Steve said.

"We have to ride them all," Marlon said.

The boys weren't the only ones who were excited. The whole eighth-grade class was thrilled. Even kids who were scared of fast rides were going.

"Marlon!" Mrs. Moore sounded mad. "What are you doing? It's time for bed."

"He'd better be sleeping," his dad said.

"Are you in bed?" his mom asked.

Marlon and Steve made silly faces. They tried not to laugh. Marlon thought his parents were downstairs.

"Um, yes." Marlon put a pillow over his face. He was cracking up.

"You'd better be," his mom said. "Or you can forget about that class trip."

The boys looked at each other. "Later," Steve said. He signed off.

"I am, Mom," Marlon said.

He pressed his recording app. Catching his mom nagging would be fun.

"We mean it, Marlon." His dad's voice was stern. "Bed. Now."

"Okay." Marlon snorted, trying not to laugh. He stopped the voice recording. He wanted to play it. Suddenly there was a knock on his door. "I'm trying to sleep!" he called.

"It's me," Ashley said.

She opened the door. Ashley was still dressed. She wore black jeans. Her black T-shirt had a front pocket. Her long black hair was in a ponytail.

"You're going to get me in trouble." Marlon pretended to be mad.

"You don't need my help doing that." Ashley laughed. "Did you take my Wite-Out?"

"Yeah, but I put it back."

"Where? Is it on my desk?"

"I think so." Marlon eyed his phone. "Maybe it's downstairs."

"You're a dweeb," Ashley said, sighing.

"Here." Marlon held up his phone. "Listen." It was the recording he'd made of their parents.

For parents, they were cool. The two rarely got angry. Unless they felt their kids did something wrong.

"You're going to get in trouble," Ashley said.

"I'm not going to play it for them. Duh." Marlon squirmed under the covers. "I'm not that lame."

"Don't sell yourself short," Ashley said. She had all the snark of a high school sophomore. "Do not record me. If I catch you …" She turned with some attitude. Then she walked out.

"You'll never know," Marlon said.

Ashley's hand snaked back inside the room. She flicked on the light switch. Marlon groaned. He would have to get out of bed to turn it off.

Chapter 2
The Theft

It was the next morning. "Play it again," Steve said.

Marlon cracked up. He pressed a button on his phone. The boys were walking to school. A few other kids walked on the sidewalk too. It was Monday. Students were dragging.

"We mean it, Marlon." It was his dad's voice. "Bed. Now."

The boys laughed.

Marlon hadn't gone to sleep. He'd

stayed up watching funny videos. Good thing his parents didn't know.

Marlon loved themed T-shirts. Today's was rad. It had an old-school Atari joystick on it.

Steve was in his usual "uniform." He wore a T-shirt and jeans. A flannel shirt hung like a jacket. It was unbuttoned. Steve's family loved to camp. The shirt was from his dad.

"You better watch it," Steve said. "Knowing your luck, they'll hear it."

"What's up?" a voice called.

Marlon and Steve turned. It was Doug Green. He was with Clark Pham. They were coming out of 7-Eleven. Both ate doughnuts.

Walden Center was on the way to school.

It was a basic strip mall. There were food shops, a Game Stop, and a pool store.

"Hey," Marlon said.

The four of them walked to school together. Marlon and Steve always hung out with Clark and Doug.

Out of all the boys, Clark was the most hip. He wore skinny jeans and tight T-shirts. Doug dressed more like Marlon. He liked wearing T-shirts from his favorite classic rock bands.

"I checked out Viper last night," Clark said. "It looks epic!"

"I just hope I don't barf," Doug said.

"If you do," Marlon said. "Do it on Thuy Le!"

The boys snickered.

Thuy could be annoying. She hadn't

wanted to go on the trip. The class should go to a museum, she said. B-O-R-I-N-G!

At school, students talked out front. Some were on their phones. Parents dropped off other kids. The parking lot was always nuts in the morning.

The campus was shaped like an open square. Most classrooms faced each other. Off to the side was the lunch area. Behind the big square was a blacktop. It had basketball and handball courts. Next to that was a large field. It had a dirt track.

Something was different today. There was a police car parked out front. Students stopped to look.

"Why are they here?" Marlon asked.

The boys walked on the campus.

"Play that app again," Steve said. He grinned. "The guys need to hear it."

Marlon tapped his phone. His parents started nagging.

Everyone cracked up.

Thuy walked past them. "Why are you guys laughing?" she asked. She always wore big dresses. They made her look frumpy. She looked older too. "Our trip to Magic Mountain is off."

"What?" the four boys said.

"Somebody stole the money." Thuy shrugged. She kept walking.

"Is she kidding?" Steve asked.

"I hope so," Marlon said.

Chapter 3
Detective Squad

It was morning break. The four boys walked to the field. They looked around. Some students played basketball. More kids sat on the blacktop.

"This is bad!" Marlon said.

Everyone seemed sad. Thuy hadn't been joking. The money for the amusement park trip had been stolen.

The trip couldn't be rescheduled. State tests would soon begin. That was more important. The trip was for fun. Testing was serious. A science fair was coming up too. The semester was packed. No way would the eighth-grade trip happen now.

"My parents paid with a check," Doug said. "Mr. Adams said they should stop payment."

"Mine paid with cash," Steve said. "No way can they get it back. It's gone for sure."

"Why would somebody steal our trip money?" Clark ate some fruit snacks.

"You think it was somebody in the office?" Steve said.

"Like a teacher?" Doug asked. "Or maybe an aide?"

"No way. A teacher wouldn't do that." Marlon took a bite of an apple. "My mom's a teacher, dude."

"Oh yeah, right. But you never know,"

Steve said. "I saw this thing on TV. Teachers stole money from a school. They did it for years. Nobody ever found out. Then one of them bought an expensive car."

"Lots of people have expensive cars. How did someone figure it out?" Clark asked.

"Because it didn't make sense. The person couldn't afford that kind of car. They didn't make a ton of money. Let's just wait." Steve opened up some crackers. "We'll know if a teacher buys a new car. Then we can tell the principal."

Principal Williams was a nice lady. She was tall. Her hair was short and curly. She smiled a lot.

"What if the principal buys a car?" Marlon asked.

His friends looked at him.

"Or what if nobody spends the money?" Marlon asked. "I want to go to Magic Mountain now."

"Who do you think stole it?" Doug asked. "Since my idea is lame."

"A student," Marlon said. "Obviously."

"Yeah," Steve said. "Someone not going on the trip."

"Maybe it was a seventh grader," Clark said.

"Who's the biggest troublemaker?" Steve asked. "I think that's key. Find them, find the money."

"If they haven't already spent it," Marlon said sadly.

The bell sounded. Morning break was over.

Students walked to their next class. Marlon, Steve, Doug, and Clark did too.

"Guys," Marlon said. "Let's meet after school. We're going to figure it out. Let's find the person who stole the money. It needs to happen fast. Maybe the trip can be saved."

Chapter 4
Suspect #1

The four boys walked home. Cars drove by as they passed Walden Center. The guys scanned the students walking by. Suspects were named.

So far nobody agreed. Who was the thief?

"What about Austin Parks?" Doug asked.

"Austin?" Marlon said. "He gets all As. Why would he steal the money?"

"Maybe he's under pressure," Doug said. "He wants to get caught."

Marlon, Steve, and Clark gave Doug a look. Doug was a great guy. But his ideas were wild. He'd once said the principal was an alien.

"It probably wasn't just one person," Clark said.

"We could be dealing with a gang," Doug said.

"I know who," Steve said. He was looking at Panda Express. Tyler Trout had just walked out. He was carrying takeout. Tyler wore a light green T-shirt and jeans. His hair grew past his ears.

"Tyler?" Marlon asked.

"Yeah," Steve said. He nodded his head.

They watched. Tyler walked over to

a red car. It was his sister's new Mustang. Kendra was talking on her phone. She had long strawberry blonde hair. The girl was pretty. Everybody thought the two were stuck-up.

"Why him?" Marlon didn't like Tyler. Still, he didn't know if he did it.

"He has no friends," Steve said. "Maybe Magic Mountain would have been tough."

"Yeah," Doug said. "If he can't have fun, nobody can."

Then Marlon remembered something. "Hey, wait! Didn't he just get a new Nintendo 3DS?"

"Yeah," Clark said. "And a huge new tablet."

"He has 50 amiibo, remember?" Marlon said. "He tried to get the cool kids to play them on his 3DS."

"How would he have the money for that?" Steve asked.

Kendra's car pulled out of Walden Center. The boys watched.

"My sister always complains about Kendra," Marlon said. "She says the girl is cold."

"Cold but hot," Steve said. "Maybe Kendra helped."

"What do you guys think?" Clark asked.

"Let's follow him," Marlon said. "We need that money back soon. Or we'll never get to go to Magic Mountain."

Chapter 5
On the Case

It was the next day. The boys started following Tyler. It began at the morning break. Tyler made his way through the campus. He didn't talk to anyone. But Tyler had his phone. What was he doing? He walked to the blacktop.

Marlon, Steve, Doug, and Clark walked 15 yards behind. They pretended to joke around.

"He's probably planning another crime," Marlon said.

"He isn't looking around," Steve said. "I don't know …"

"Who is he texting?" Clark asked.

"His bank?" Doug said, snorting. "It's called money laundering. I heard about it on *Pawn Stars*."

Tyler sat down on the grass. His eyes never left his phone. The bell sounded.

"Well," Doug said. "That was a waste."

"What do you mean?" Marlon asked.

"All he did was send texts," Doug said.

"This is detective work," Marlon said. "It takes time to build a case."

"Yeah," Steve said. "He's probably just chillin'. He doesn't want to draw attention to himself."

"Now he can plan another job," Clark said.

Lunch was the same. Tyler sat on the field. His eyes were glued to his phone. The boys decided to follow him after school.

Tyler rode a cool mountain bike. It was black with green pedals.

Doug and Clark had brought their bikes. Steve and Marlon rode on the handlebars. Tyler rode through the busy school parking lot. The boys followed. Tyler didn't seem to notice.

"Don't peddle so fast," Marlon said.

"We don't want to lose him," Steve said.

They eventually ended up in Walden Heights. This was the richest part of Walden Lane. The houses were huge. They looked like mansions. There were expensive cars in every driveway.

Tyler turned down a street. He stopped at the largest house. Doug and Clark stopped pedaling. They didn't want Tyler to see them.

There was a huge black SUV in Tyler's driveway. Kendra's red Mustang was parked next to it.

"Guys," Steve said. He took out his phone. "I don't think he's our thief."

"Why?" Marlon asked.

"Look at his house," Clark said. "He's rich."

"Yeah," Doug said. "He doesn't need the money. His parents probably buy him everything he wants."

"I just looked up his dad," Steve said. He held up his phone. "He is Daniel Trout. The dude is one of the richest in Walden Lane."

It was Wednesday morning. Everyone rode their bikes to school. Steve and Marlon met at the park. "We got him!" Steve said.

"Who?" Marlon asked.

He hadn't spoken to the guys since last night. Their search had been a dead end. Marlon had gone home. He'd done his homework. Then he ate dinner. He killed time playing video games. Who was the thief?

"Colton Banes," Steve said. "It makes total sense."

"Huh? It does?" Marlon didn't know anything about Colton. He did have a bad reputation. The guy was known as a troublemaker.

"Colton's new at school. But he's already got a bad rep," Steve said. "He's only been here four months. He was suspended once. Nobody likes him. He has even less friends than Tyler."

"I don't know," Marlon said.

"What's not to know?"

Marlon couldn't put his finger on it. Something felt wrong.

Chapter 6
Suspect #2

The boys followed Colton after school. It was a complete 180. Colton's life didn't even come close to Tyler's.

Colton walked home in the opposite direction. He lived on the south side. It was a sketchy area. That part of Walden Lane was rundown. There was a lot of graffiti. Marlon heard there was more crime too.

Colton walked up to an area called Parkhurst. It was an old apartment complex.

There was so much trash. People were standing around. Some had phones. Others just watched cars drive by. Everyone had one thing in common. They looked rough.

"I didn't know he lived here," Doug said.

Suddenly a white truck pulled up. The driver was a man. He had an angry look on his face. The man wore a red baseball cap. He had a mustache. The man waved to Colton. Colton quickly got into the truck. They took off.

"Should we follow them?" Steve asked.

"Nah," Marlon said. "We can't pedal that fast."

The boys rode toward home. They had questions. Who was that guy? Why did Colton get into that truck?

They were pretty sure Colton was the

thief. He was a troublemaker. His neighborhood was ratty. He didn't seem to have money. It all made sense.

Marlon had his doubts.

Marlon was alone. He was close to home when he saw Tyler. Tyler was riding his bike too. He carried a blue bag. It dangled from the handlebars. Tyler was also talking on his phone. He didn't notice Marlon.

Marlon followed him. He didn't want Tyler to spot him. So he hid behind a car.

The boys were in a parking lot. The lot was for Vista Center. This was a smaller strip mall. It was in a decent part of town. There were only three services. A Taco Bell that was always busy. Plus a gas station and car wash. Cars were always coming and going.

Marlon watched Tyler. He was talking to a tall man. The man was dressed in black. He looked at what was inside Tyler's blue bag. Was it money? Marlon was too far away to tell. The man gave Tyler a brown box.

Then Tyler quickly pedaled away. The man got in his car and drove off.

Marlon didn't follow Tyler. But he sure was suspicious. Should he mention it to the guys? He decided not to tell them. They were pretty set on Colton.

Chapter 7
Marlon Moore, PI

It was date night. Their parents were out. Marlon and Ashley sat in the kitchen. Ashley had ordered a pizza.

She put out plates. Marlon got drinks.

Date night was great. It was cool being home alone. But Ashley was still in charge. It bummed Marlon out sometimes. As far as big sisters went, she was cool.

"Did you see what Tyler gave him?" Ashley put a piece of pizza on her plate. "You don't know what was inside the box."

"Tyler gave him money," Marlon said. "I can feel it."

"So what?" Ashley said. "Money changes hands all the time."

"But why some random parking lot? Why that guy? How does Tyler know him?"

"Maybe it was money for charity. It could be anything. The Trouts are rich. And *so* stuck-up."

"It was the Magic Mountain money. I just know it." Marlon took a bite of pizza.

Ashley rolled her eyes. She loved her brother. But the kid had a big imagination. "Marlon—"

"You'll see I'm right. Watch." Marlon picked up his pizza and drink. He walked out of the kitchen.

"Don't be mad!" Ashley called.

He didn't respond. Marlon went upstairs to his room. It was bad when adults didn't believe kids. His sister's disbelief was worse.

Thursday passed. There was no news. Now it was Friday morning. Marlon met Steve at the park. The boys rode their bikes again. "Colton stole the money," Steve said.

"How can you be so sure?" Marlon asked.

"Wait till you talk to Clark and Doug," Steve said. He smiled. "They have hard evidence."

The two rode to school. They met up with the other boys. Clark showed Marlon his phone. There were pictures of Colton. He was at Target. Colton was with two boys.

"He's shopping with his friends," Marlon said. "Who cares? This means nothing."

Clark smiled. Then he swiped past a few more pictures. Colton was buying video games.

"He bought a game for each of his friends," Doug said. "The newest versions."

"*Battlefield*," Clark said.

"*Fight Night. Halo*," Steve added. "He lives in the hood. Nobody from Parkhurst has money."

"That doesn't prove anything. You don't know he stole the money," Marlon said. "Maybe the games are on sale."

"You think he didn't do it. Why?" Clark asked.

"It seems too obvious. He's poor," Marlon said. "So he steals."

The guys looked at Marlon.

"Well," Steve said. "It's almost the weekend. We're going to follow him. There will be more pictures. We'll get the evidence. The principal will see it on Monday."

Chapter 8
More Proof

Nobody had time to follow Colton later. Steve was going to his uncle's house. His uncle lived in LA. It was an hour from Walden Lane.

Steve loved going there. His uncle worked in the movie business. He wrote screenplays. His house was huge. Steve hadn't seen any of his uncle's movies. But he enjoyed his stories.

Clark's sister had a piano recital. In

his family the piano was a big deal. They would dress up for the recital. Afterward, they always went out to eat.

Doug was Jewish. His family went to the synagogue on Friday nights. Doug usually didn't get to see his friends until Saturday evening.

Marlon was free. It was decided. He would follow Tyler. School was over. He got his bike. Tyler wasn't too far ahead.

Tyler rode fast. He was yelling at someone on his phone. Marlon couldn't hear the words.

Tyler's blue bag dangled from the handlebars. Marlon tried to ride closer. He didn't want to blow his cover.

Then something amazing happened. The blue bag fell to the ground.

Marlon couldn't believe it. Tyler kept on riding. He was too into his conversation. Cool! He didn't even notice.

Now was the time! Marlon raced over to it. He quickly stopped his bike. Then he grabbed the bag. There were some papers inside. Marlon looked closer.

The papers were checks!

His heart raced. Were these the checks from the school burglary?

"Hey!" Tyler yelled. He dropped his bike to the ground. His face was scrunched up in anger. The bag was ripped from Marlon's hand. "What are you doing?" he screamed.

Then Tyler pushed Marlon.

"You dropped your bag," Marlon said. "I was going to give it back to you."

Tyler frowned. He looked inside. "Whatever," he said. He turned away. "Mind your own business." Then he rode off.

It was an hour later. Ashley was in the bathroom. She held some mascara in her hand. On Fridays she usually hung out with Kayla Flores. Kayla was her best friend. The two girls had met in third grade. Tonight they were going to the movies.

"Are you sure?" Ashley asked. "Were there really checks in that bag?"

"Positive," Marlon said. "Do you believe me now? Colton didn't do it."

"That doesn't mean Tyler did. You don't know what the checks were for. If you had gotten a better look—"

"I couldn't," Marlon said. "He grabbed

the bag. Come on, Ashley. I need your help. The guys will narc on Colton. But he's innocent."

"Help?" Ashley eyed him. "How? What can I do?"

"I don't know. I'm going to keep watching Tyler. I want to film him. Can you help? What are you doing tomorrow?"

"I've got a track meet. It's all day," she said.

"Fine," he said. "After that?"

"Maybe."

Marlon thought about calling Steve. He wanted to tell him about the checks. But he had a bigger goal. Colton didn't do it. And Marlon wanted to prove it.

He decided not to call anyone. Marlon had another idea.

Chapter 9
The Chase

Marlon got up early Saturday morning. He rode over to Parkhurst. Marlon wanted to follow Colton.

What will I say to him? Will I tell him the guys think he's a crook?

That could cause so many problems. Steve, Clark, and Doug would be mad at him. They wouldn't like his undercover operation. He'd done it behind their backs. The guys were so sure Colton was the thief.

And what if Colton did it? Colton

wouldn't tell. And where was the money? Maybe it was gone. The trip would be off for sure.

Marlon stood across the street from Parkhurst. A strip mall was behind him. It had a Mexican restaurant. A self-service laundry was already busy. There was also a cell phone fix-it place.

Marlon sat on a bench. He studied his phone. The screen was smudged. That's when he realized something.

Parkhurst was in a rundown area. That didn't mean it was the hood. People walked by. They smiled at him. He didn't feel unsafe.

People in Walden Lane didn't like Parkhurst. But it wasn't a bad place. It was just different. Like Colton.

Colton acted tough. He was different.

Kids at school didn't know him well. But that didn't mean he was bad.

A few minutes passed. A boy came out of the complex. He wore jeans and a white T-shirt. It was Colton. He stood on the street. What was he looking for? Every 10 seconds he checked his phone.

Then the man in the white truck pulled up. Colton smiled. He got in. The man was smiling too. Colton gave him a hug. They drove off.

Marlon did his best to keep up. It was hard. His bike was old.

The truck drove on for 10 minutes. Marlon huffed and puffed. It took so much effort. He had to stay close. Luckily every light was red.

The truck pulled into a construction site. It was closer to Marlon's house. A steel frame rose into the sky. Was it a future office building? It looked like it.

Marlon stopped by some trees. He could still see the truck.

Colton and the stranger got out. They walked toward the site. The man had on the same clothes as Colton. He also wore tan boots.

The two were laughing. The man put his arm around Colton. Other people at the site walked up to them. Everyone dressed alike. Tool belts hung from their waists.

The men shook hands. They high-fived Colton.

"Your son is almost taller than you!" A man with a big beard laughed. Then everyone laughed.

Duh! How could Marlon miss the clues. The stranger was Colton's dad!

One of the men had cash in his hand. He gave it to Colton's dad. The men spoke. Then father and son turned to leave. They walked back to the truck. Colton's dad gave him some bills. Colton hugged him.

Marlon raced away on his bike. His head was spinning. He took out his phone. It was time to call Steve.

Ugh! I am so dumb. That is his dad. He gave Colton money. Colton must have helped the crew. That's why he had cash at Target. He was sharing it with his friends. That's how he bought those games.

Then Marlon felt guilty. Nobody had given Colton a chance at school. Maybe the guy was nice.

Marlon had to tell Steve. He looked down at his phone. Everyone had to know about it. Colton was innocent.

A car came out of nowhere. It was a red Mustang. Marlon swerved. The car almost hit him. He tried not to wipe out.

Then he realized who was in the car. It was Tyler and Kendra.

Oh no! They were after him!

Chapter 10
Saved

Marlon rode quickly toward Walden Park. There was a large hill. He pedaled hard. The hill sloped down into the park. There was a playground. Across from that was a trail. It led into a wilderness area.

Marlon looked behind him. Kendra was still following! Why? The street would end soon. There was just a parking lot.

Marlon pedaled fast. Now he was at the bottom of the hill. His bike hit a patch of mud. The bike swayed and wobbled. He tried to regain control. But he crashed. He rolled for a few feet. Pain shot up his leg.

He grabbed his leg as he stood. Kendra's car had just totaled his bike. It flew a few feet and landed. Marlon wanted to run. But he simply couldn't. His leg hurt too much.

Kendra turned off her car. She and Tyler got out. They surrounded him.

"What are you doing? I could have been killed!" Marlon screamed.

"Why have you been following me?" Tyler yelled.

"What? I wasn't …" He stalled. Reaching into his pocket, Marlon found his phone. He pressed what he hoped was the voice record app.

"Liar!" Tyler said. "You followed me yesterday. In fact, I've seen you all week. What gives?"

"We know about you," Kendra said. "We know about your family."

"Yeah," Tyler said. "Do you want your parents to lose their jobs?"

"Wait, what? You guys can't do that!" Marlon was super scared.

"Your mom is a teacher." Kendra smiled slyly. "Your dad works for the city. Our dad can make it all go away. Like that!" She snapped her fingers.

"Stop being nosy," Tyler said. "Stop spreading lies."

"But you stole the money!" Marlon said. "You guys are rich. Why do you need—"

"Because we can! Okay?" Kendra yelled. "It's none of your business."

"And we're not saying more," Tyler said. "Because we didn't do anything. Got it?"

They stared at Marlon. He knew the two could hurt him. But it just wasn't fair.

"You ruined the trip," Marlon said. "Why ruin it for everyone?"

"Wouldn't you like to know." Tyler smirked. "I'm so happy I took that trip away from you."

"Shhh, Tyler," Kendra said. "Everybody in Walden Lane is unfriendly. They've never accepted us. Never will. There's no point talking to him."

Marlon realized something. Tyler and Kendra felt left out. That's why they stole the money. They weren't happy. So they made sure nobody was happy.

The kids heard a police siren. There was a patrol car at the top of the hill. It slowly moved forward. Its lights flashed. Then it stopped. A few officers got out of the car. They quickly moved toward them.

"What's going on here?" an officer said.

"He stole something from my car," Kendra lied.

"That's why we had to chase him," Tyler said.

"That's a lie!" Marlon said. "I didn't do anything."

"Stop lying!" Tyler snapped.

"Officer, our father is Daniel Trout," Kendra said. "Let me call him." She took out her phone.

Marlon blinked. He couldn't believe it. Ashley got out of the patrol car! She ran over to them. "Are you okay?" she asked.

"Yeah, I'm fine." Marlon took out his

phone. He looked at it. "Officers, I need you to listen to something."

Yes! He had pressed the right button. Marlon played the recorded conversation. Tyler and Kendra's every word was on the record. Now it was Marlon's turn to smirk.

The police knew Marlon was innocent. Now they also knew who stole the eighth-grade trip money.

Two sets of parents arrived on the scene. The Moores looked worried. So did the Trouts.

The police had Marlon's phone. They played the recording. Marlon was relieved. He wasn't in any trouble. Sadly, Kendra and Tyler were. Big-time!

"Thanks for believing me," Marlon said. He hugged Ashley.

"You tell stories sometimes," Ashley

said. "Not this time, though. I had a feeling you were telling the truth."

It was two weeks later. Marlon and Steve were sitting on a school bus. Behind them were Doug and Clark. The bus was filled with eighth graders. They were going to Magic Mountain. The trip had been saved. Mr. Trout had paid for the entire thing.

Kendra and Tyler were in trouble. It was their first offense. Their dad had made a deal. The two didn't go to juvenile detention. Instead, they each had community service. Both needed counseling too. Kendra was suspended from the high school. Tyler was suspended too.

As they drove, Marlon laughed. Steve had shown him a meme on his phone. Marlon looked over at Colton. He was sitting a few rows back. Did Colton have anybody to hang with at the park? Did he feel left out?

Marlon knew what he needed to do. He nudged Steve. "Hey," he said. "Let's ask Colton to hang with us today."

"Do you think he will?" Steve asked.

"Sure," Marlon said. "We at least need to ask. Otherwise, we'll never know."

It was decided. Colton would hang with Marlon's crew. The Viper was waiting for them. Seven loops and 3,830 feet of pure terror. Awesome!